THE BOOKSHOP OF DESIRE

ELIZA FINCH

1

The sun dipped low in the sky, casting long shadows over the cobblestone streets of Victorian-era London. Mary stood before the bookshop she had inherited from her late uncle, its weathered sign swaying gently above her head. The scent of aged leather and musty paper filled her nostrils as she pushed open the door.

This bookshop held a special place in her heart, having spent many hours here under her uncle's guidance, learning about the world beyond the rigid constraints of her conservative upbringing.

As Mary began to peruse the shelves, she couldn't help but replay the words of her family over and over in her head.

"Is it proper for a young lady to be running a bookshop?" whispered her Aunt Agnes, her voice dripping with disapproval. "Especially one that sells such... scandalous material?"

"Her uncle's dying wish was for her to have this shop," replied her father reluctantly, his voice heavy with disappointment. "We cannot go against his wishes, no matter how unseemly it may appear."

Remembering this conversation, Mary clenched her fists,

desperately trying to forget their judgmental whispers. She knew they would never understand her passion for literature, nor her growing curiosity about the sensual pleasures hinted at within the pages of the novels she discovered in her uncle's secret collection.

Lost in her thoughts, Mary's fingers trailed along the spines of the books, feeling each one as if it held a secret waiting to be unraveled. Her heart quickened as she imagined the forbidden knowledge and hidden desires that lay within their pages.

As she continued her exploration, her eyes fell upon a small, leather-bound book tucked away on a dusty shelf. The title, "The Enigmatic Seduction," was etched in gold letters across its cover. Intrigued, Mary carefully removed it from its resting place, her hands trembling with anticipation.

She settled into a worn armchair near the fireplace, its crackling flames casting a warm glow around the room. With bated breath, she began to read, her heart pounding in her chest.

The words on the pages transported Mary to a world unlike any she had known. The story unfolded before her eyes, weaving an intricate tale of passion, desire, and forbidden love.

Her pulse raced with each scandalous encounter described in vivid detail, as if the characters themselves were whispering their secrets directly into her ear. Mary's cheeks flushed with a mixture of excitement and guilt, her hand involuntarily tracing the curves of her own body as she lost herself in the narrative.

She had read love stories before, but none had evoked such a visceral response within her. The words ignited a fire deep within her core, awakening a hunger she never knew existed. As the story delved deeper into the depths of pleasure and surrender, Mary found herself yearning for something more.

With trembling hands, she continued reading, finding solace in the anonymity of her desires. The book became her confidante, a gateway to a world that beckoned her to shed the restraints of society and embrace her own hidden passions. Each page turned was a step towards liberation, towards exploration.

Suddenly she was startled by a voice.

"Hello? Is anyone here?" Mary was so deeply entrenched in her book that she had failed to notice a customer had entered the store. It was a man, quite handsome, dressed in a tailored suit that accentuated his broad shoulders. His dark hair was neatly combed, framing a face that exuded an air of confidence.

Startled, Mary snapped the book shut, the forbidden words now hidden from view. She hastily stood up, her cheeks flushed with embarrassment.

"I apologize, sir. I didn't realize there was anyone else in the shop," she stammered, her voice betraying her unease.

The man's eyes sparkled with amusement as he looked at Mary, his lips curling into a mischievous smile. "No need to apologize, my dear. It seems I have interrupted quite an engrossing read," he replied, his voice smooth as velvet.

Mary's heart skipped a beat at the sound of his voice. She found herself captivated by his presence, drawn to the energy that seemed to radiate from him.

"I must confess," he continued, taking a step closer, "I am quite intrigued by what had captured your attention so intensely. May I ask what book had you so enthralled?"

Mary hesitated for a moment, unsure whether to reveal her secret indulgence. But there was something about this stranger that made her feel strangely uninhibited, as if she could freely express her desires without fear of judgment.

"I...I was reading 'The Enigmatic Seduction,'" she admitted, her voice barely above a whisper.

A flicker of surprise crossed the man's face before he smiled knowingly. "Ah, a tale of passion and intrigue," he murmured, his voice dripping with seduction. "A fitting choice for such a captivating woman as yourself."

Mary felt her cheeks redden even more at the compliment. She glanced down at the book still clutched tightly in her hand, the pages practically burning with desire.

"Do you enjoy literature of this nature?" she asked cautiously, unable to resist testing the waters.

His eyes sparkled with an intensity that sent shivers down Mary's spine. "Indeed," he replied, his voice low and filled with a hint of mischief. "I find that stories that explore the depths of passion and desire are the most captivating. They allow us to delve into the forbidden, to explore hidden desires that society often tries to suppress."

Mary's heart raced at his words, her curiosity growing stronger with each passing second. This man, with his alluring presence and shared appreciation for provocative literature, seemed to understand her in ways no one else did.

"Would you care to share your thoughts on 'The Enigmatic Seduction'?" he asked, his eyes fixed on Mary's face as if he could read her innermost desires.

Mary hesitated for a moment, her mind racing with conflicting emotions. The thought of discussing the intimate details of the book with a stranger felt scandalous, yet undeniably thrilling. Casting aside her inhibitions, she nodded slowly.

"I... I would like that," she replied, her voice barely above a whisper. "There is a certain allure in discussing such passions with someone who truly understands."

The man's smile deepened, and he extended a hand towards Mary. "Then, allow me to properly introduce myself. My name is Henry. May I ask your name?"

"Mary," she whispered.

"Well, Mary my dear, let us retire to a more comfortable setting," he said, his voice now a velvety purr. "I know of a nearby café where we can indulge in our mutual appreciation for literature and explore the depths of our desires further."

Mary hesitated for only a moment before deciding to go for it. She quickly closed up shop. Then she placed her hand in his, feeling an electric current surge through her veins at the simple touch. With a gentle squeeze, the man led her out of the bookshop into the dimly lit streets of London.

As they walked side by side, Mary wondered at the magnetism she felt towards this mysterious stranger. It was as if their shared love for literature had forged an unspoken connection between them. Her heart pounded in her chest, and she found herself yearning for what lay ahead.

2

The warm glow of the gas lamps flickered on the glossy marble walls, casting an amber hue over the patrons of the local café. The air was thick with the scent of freshly brewed coffee and rich tobacco smoke, a heady aroma that teased the senses and heightened one's awareness of the intimate surroundings. Couples huddled together in secluded corners, their whispers barely audible above the low hum of conversation and the clink of china cups against saucers.

"Shall we sit over here?" Henry asked, pointing to a table in the corner. Mary sat in the seat that Henry pulled out for her while he took a seat opposite her.

"So tell me, Mary, the author of your book has quite the talent for capturing the raw essence of desire, wouldn't you agree?"

"Absolutely," Mary nodded, her heart pounding in her chest as she played nervously with the edge of the book. "It's...awakening something within me, stirring up these longings I've never experienced before."

Henry leaned forward slightly, his piercing blue eyes searching hers. "And what is it about these particular scenes that resonates so strongly with you, Mary?"

She hesitated, feeling exposed under his intense gaze. But there was something about the way he spoke, his voice like velvet, that made her want to open up to him.

"Perhaps it's the freedom," she confessed, her voice barely more than a whisper. "The ability to explore one's most primal desires without restraint, to be completely vulnerable and yet fully in control."

"Ah," Henry murmured, a knowing smile playing on his lips. "A delicate balance, to be sure. And yet, when achieved, it can lead to the most exquisite pleasures."

As they continued their conversation, the connection between them grew stronger, their chemistry undeniable. They leaned closer together, their hands occasionally brushing against each other, sending shivers down their spines.

"Tell me, Mary," Henry inquired, his voice low and sultry. "Have you ever considered exploring these desires yourself? Experiencing the delicate dance between pleasure and pain, dominance and submission?"

Mary's breath hitched as she met his gaze, seeing the fire burning in his eyes. A part of her wanted to shy away, retreat to the safety of her familiar world. But another part, the part awakened by the words in the book and the man sitting before her, yearned for more.

"I...I've thought about it," she admitted, her voice trembling with anticipation. "But I wouldn't know where to begin."

"Then allow me to guide you," Henry offered, his hand reaching across the table to gently caress hers. "Together, we can explore the depths of your desires, push the boundaries of pleasure, and awaken the true potential within you."

Mary felt a shudder run through her entire being as she

looked into Henry's eyes, her decision made. She was ready to embark on this journey, to surrender herself to the unknown and experience the world of passion that lay just beyond the pages of her book.

"Mary, your curiosity and intelligence are truly captivating," Henry said, his voice tinged with admiration. "Your willingness to discuss such taboo topics openly is a rarity, and I must admit, it intrigues me."

"Thank you, Henry," Mary replied, feeling her cheeks flush with warmth. "I've always believed that knowledge is power, and that there should be no shame in exploring the depths of our desires. I've just never had the opportunity."

"Indeed," he agreed, leaning forward slightly, his eyes locked on hers. "And it's that fearless pursuit of knowledge that makes you an ideal candidate for the journey I'm offering. I believe that together, we can unlock sensations and experiences you've never even dreamed of."

"Is that so?" Mary asked, a coy smile playing at the corner of her lips. "And just what kind of experiences are we talking about?"

"Ah, my dear," Henry said, his voice dropping to a tantalizing whisper. "That would be telling, wouldn't it? But let's just say that the ropes binding the characters in your book are but a mere taste of the heights of pleasure we could reach."

"Ropes?" Mary echoed, feeling a thrill run through her at the thought. "So, you're well-versed in the art of...restraint, then?"

"More than well-versed, my darling," Henry assured her, his fingertips tracing delicate patterns on the back of her hand in a sensual caress. "And that's just one aspect of the many exquisite forms of pleasure we can explore together."

"Such as?" Mary couldn't help but ask, her heart racing at the prospect of delving into this forbidden world with Henry as her guide.

"Perhaps I could demonstrate some of those pleasures for you," Henry suggested, his gaze intense and unwavering. "Would you like that, Mary? To have your senses awakened and your body brought to the brink of ecstasy, only to be pulled back and guided further into uncharted territory?"

"Y-yes," Mary stammered, her breath catching in her throat at the boldness of his proposition. "I think I would very much like that."

"Excellent," Henry said, his fingers now entwined with hers, his grip firm yet gentle. "Then let us embark on this journey together, Mary. And I promise you, it will be a voyage unlike any you've ever experienced before."

As their eyes met once more, Mary felt the heat of their mutual desire igniting within her, fueling her anticipation for the erotic explorations that lay ahead. With Henry by her side, she was ready to embrace the unknown and surrender herself to the intoxicating world of sensual pleasure that awaited them both.

"Tell me, Mary," Henry murmured, leaning closer as his breath caressed her cheek, "have you ever experienced the sensation of silk against your skin? The way it glides and clings, leaving shivers in its wake?"

"Only in my dreams," she admitted, her voice low and husky. She could feel the heat radiating off him, stoking the embers of her desire until they threatened to become a consuming fire.

"Or perhaps the thrill of leather?" he continued, his fingertips tracing tantalizing circles on the back of her hand. "Its supple strength can be quite...binding."

"Binding?" Mary repeated, her pulse quickening at the implications of his words. Was he suggesting what she thought he was?

"Indeed," he confirmed, a wicked smile dancing on his lips. "Imagine, if you will, the gentle constriction of a collar around your throat, or the snug embrace of cuffs upon your wrists – the sweet surrender of control." His voice was a siren's song, drawing her further into uncharted waters with each seductive syllable.

"Control is overrated," she whispered, unable to resist the allure of his proposition. Her chest rose and fell with each ragged breath, her body aching for the release he promised.

"Ah, but that's where you're mistaken, my dear," he countered, his gaze dark and predatory as it locked onto hers. "You see, in the hands of a skilled lover, control becomes an exquisite tool – one that can coax the most divine pleasures from even the most reticent of participants."

As he spoke, he brushed a stray lock of hair from her face, his touch electrifying her senses and causing her to shudder involuntarily. This man, this enigmatic stranger who had so effortlessly ensnared her attention and inflamed her desires, was offering her the opportunity to explore the forbidden depths of her own sensuality – an invitation she found impossible to resist.

"Show me," she urged, her eyes pleading with him to guide her on this perilous path to ecstasy. "Teach me the secrets hidden within these pages, and let me taste the pleasures of which they speak."

"Patience, my sweet," he cautioned, his fingers entwining with hers once more as he leaned in to brush a feather-light kiss against her temple. "The journey we are about to embark upon is not one to be rushed. It will require trust, communication, and above all, an open mind." He paused, allowing his words to sink in before adding, "Are you prepared for that, Mary?"

"More than you can know," she breathed, her resolve solidifying in the face of his unwavering confidence.

"Then let us begin," he declared, his eyes alight with anticipation as they rose from their seats and exited the café together. As they stepped out into the bustling streets of Victorian-era London, Mary knew that her life was about to change forever – and she couldn't wait to see what lay in store.

As Mary and Henry walked arm in arm along the cobblestone streets, the golden light of the setting sun cast long shadows that seemed to dance with their every step. The promise of the night ahead was palpable, as if the very air around them thrummed with anticipation.

"Mary," Henry murmured, his voice low and intimate as he leaned in close, "there will be moments when you may feel overwhelmed or uncertain. But I want you to remember that you have the power to shape your own desires, to mold them into something exquisite and unique."

"Even when it feels... taboo?" she asked hesitantly, her cheeks flushed with a mixture of embarrassment and excitement.

"Especially then," he replied, his eyes dark and intense. "Those are the moments when you'll discover the true depths of your passion, the hidden corners of your soul where pleasure and pain intertwine."

As they continued on, Mary couldn't help but notice the way her fellow Londoners seemed to carry on with their lives, blissfully unaware of the tumultuous journey that lay before her. A journey that would strip away the constraints of society, leaving her free to explore the most primal aspects of her being.

"Will it be difficult?" she asked, her voice trembling slightly as she considered the magnitude of what she was about to undertake.

"Of course," Henry answered honestly, his fingers tightening around hers in a reassuring grip. "But the challenges we face only serve to heighten the satisfaction of our conquests. And I promise you, Mary, there is no greater reward than the ecstasy that awaits you at the end of this path."

As they turned down a narrow alleyway, the flickering glow of gaslights casting eerie shadows on the damp brick walls, Mary felt a shiver of apprehension run down her spine.

"Are you still with me?" Henry asked softly, his gaze searching hers for any sign of doubt or hesitation.

"Always," she whispered, her heart swelling with determination as she faced the unknown with courage and resolve. "I am ready for whatever lies ahead."

"Good," he replied, a wicked grin spreading across his handsome face. "Because, my dear, we have only just begun."

3
_____

The night air was thick with anticipation as Mary and Henry left the dimly lit streets behind, making their way towards Henry's London home. The gas lights cast a sensual glow over the couple, their bodies pressed against each other as they walked hand in hand.

"Are you ready for this?" Henry asked, his voice low and sultry as he stole a glance at Mary, her usually innocent eyes now filled with desire.

"More than anything," she replied breathlessly, feeling her heart race as they reached the entrance of his home.

As they stepped inside, the warmth enveloped them, its opulence a stark contrast to the gritty streets outside. Henry led Mary into a sitting room, his fingers lingering on her lower back, sending shivers down her spine.

"Your home is lovely," Mary admitted, trying to control her breathing as Henry closed the door, sealing them off from the world outside.

"Wait until you see what I have in store for you," Henry whispered, his lips grazing her earlobe, causing her knees to weaken.

The darkened room was illuminated only by flickering candle-light, casting seductive shadows on the walls. He guided her through the home, his arm wrapped protectively around her waist.

"Have a seat," Henry instructed, gesturing towards the sofa. "I'll be right back."

As Mary perched herself on the edge of the cushioned surface, she felt a mixture of excitement and apprehension. She knew that Henry was experienced in the world of pleasure, having confessed his passion for BDSM and other erotic pursuits. It thrilled her to think that she would soon be immersed in these forbidden experiences under his guidance.

"Relax, Mary," Henry said soothingly as he returned from another room, his hands holding something she couldn't quite make out. The flickering candlelight danced across his face, highlighting the intensity in his eyes. "Tonight, we explore our desires together."

"Show me," Mary whispered, her voice barely audible over the pounding of her heart.

"Close your eyes, Mary," Henry instructed, his voice low and commanding. Obediently, she shut her eyelids, the darkness enveloping her senses. She felt the soft fabric of a blindfold being tied around her head, the knot snug against her skin.

"Trust me," he whispered into her ear, sending shivers down her spine. "Now, your other senses will be heightened, making every touch more intense."

Mary's breath hitched as she felt the heat of Henry's body near hers. Her anticipation surged, the unknown thrilling her. As she sat there on the edge of the sofa, waiting for what was to come, she could hear the subtle sounds of their surroundings – the crackle of the fireplace, the rustle of fabric as Henry moved about the room.

"Stand up," he ordered, his tone gentle yet firm. Mary rose from the cushion, feeling vulnerable yet excited in her state of sensory deprivation.

Henry's hands found her shoulders, gently stroking her collarbones before slowly gliding down her arms. The sensation sparked a fire within her, goosebumps erupting on her skin. He traced the curve of her waist, his fingertips teasing the back of her dress, eliciting a quiet gasp from her lips.

"Let me undress you, piece by piece," he murmured, his breath hot against her neck. He carefully unbuttoned her dress, taking his time to savor the reveal of her body. As the fabric fell away, he grazed his fingers over her undergarments. He drew lazy circles around her nipples, which were already hardening in response. A moan escaped Mary's mouth, the ache for more growing stronger.

"Beautiful," he praised, his voice darkened with lust. His hands continued their exploration, traveling lower. Methodically, he untied her undergarments, allowing the fabric to pool around her ankles. As she stepped out of the garment, she felt a newfound freedom – her body exposed and vulnerable, yet empowered.

"Tell me what you're feeling," Henry demanded, eager to hear her thoughts.

"Desire," Mary breathed, her voice trembling with need. "But... also fear."

"Good," he replied, a hint of a smile in his voice. "Fear can fuel passion, and tonight, we'll conquer that fear together."

"Are you ready to take this further, Mary?" Henry asked, his voice laced with desire and authority.

"Y-yes," she stammered, surrendering herself to the unknown.

"Good. Trust me," he whispered, as he gently guided her to the bed. There, he began to fasten soft leather restraints around her wrists and ankles, securing her limbs to the bedposts. The sound of the buckles clicking into place sent shivers down Mary's spine, a thrilling mix of fear and anticipation coursing through her veins.

"Your body is mine to control now," Henry declared, his tone commanding yet reassuring. "Remember your safe word if it gets too intense."

"Green," Mary murmured, committing the word to memory.

"Excellent." A wicked grin spread across his face, as he reached for a leather paddle from the nearby dresser. "Let's begin."

The first crack of the paddle against her skin caught Mary off guard, the sharp sting of pain followed by a gentle caress of his fingers. She gasped at the sensation, her body instinctively arching towards him.

"Did that hurt?" Henry inquired, his breath hot on her earlobe.

"Y-yes," Mary stuttered, feeling exposed and vulnerable in her bound state.

"Good. Pain can be a powerful aphrodisiac when wielded correctly," he explained, his words punctuated by another swat, this time harder and more deliberate.

"Ah!" Mary cried out, her mind struggling to reconcile the conflicting emotions coursing through her – the undeniable pleasure mingling with the searing pain.

"Tell me how it feels," he demanded, his voice firm yet tender.

"Intense... overwhelming... but I want more," she admitted, surprising even herself with her newfound craving.

"Very well," Henry replied, a note of satisfaction in his voice. He continued to spank her, each strike sending a shockwave of pleasure-pain through her body. As the heat on her skin built, so did the fire within her – an uncontrollable inferno of desire that consumed every inch of her being.

"Please... touch me," Mary begged, her voice desperate and raw.

"Such a greedy little thing," he teased, his fingers ghosting over her slick folds before finally granting her the contact she craved. The sensation was electric – an explosion of ecstasy that left her trembling and gasping for breath.

"Remember, I am in control here," Henry reminded her, his voice both soothing and domineering. "And tonight, you will learn the art of submission."

"Yes, Sir," Mary answered, her voice barely a whisper as she surrendered herself completely to his mastery.

"Are you ready for the next lesson, Mary?" Henry asked, his breath hot against her ear.

"Y-yes, Sir," she stammered, anticipation tingling through her veins.

"Good," Henry whispered, his eyes dark with desire.

He released the restraints on Mary and removed the blindfold.

"Now, I want you to kneel before me and learn the art of oral pleasure."

As Mary sank to her knees before him, she felt a mix of excitement and trepidation. She had read about such acts, but had never experienced it herself. Her heart pounded in her chest as she looked up at Henry, seeking guidance.

"Begin by teasing the tip with your tongue," he instructed, his voice husky with arousal. "Then slowly work your way around the shaft, using your lips, your tongue, and even your hands to stroke and massage."

Mary tentatively followed his instructions, finding her own arousal growing as she explored this new territory. The taste, the texture, and the moans escaping Henry's lips all fueled her desire to please him.

"Fuck, that's good," Henry groaned, his fingers gripping her hair gently but firmly. "Now, take me deeper, my dear. Let yourself savor every inch."

As Mary took him further into her mouth, she marveled at the power she held over this man who had dominated her so thoroughly earlier in the evening. She reveled in the pleasure she was giving him, feeling her body respond to his escalating excitement.

"Enough teasing, my love," Henry declared, pulling her to her feet. "It's time for us to truly become one."

Their eyes locked as they stood facing each other, two bodies consumed by their passion, their craving for one another nearly unbearable. In a swift movement, Henry lifted Mary onto a nearby table, spreading her legs wide as he positioned himself between them.

"Are you ready for this, Mary?" he asked, his voice thick with lust.

"Please, Sir," she begged, her body trembling with anticipation. "I need you inside me."

With that, Henry plunged into her, eliciting a gasp of pleasure from both of them. Their bodies moved in sync, each thrust driving them closer to the edge. Mary's mind was a whirlwind of sensations: the feeling of being filled, the delicious friction as he pulled out and pushed back in, and the indescribable connection between them.

"Touch yourself, Mary," Henry commanded, his voice rough with desire. "I want to see you come undone while I fuck you."

Her fingers traced their way down her body, seeking the sweet spot that would send her over the edge. As she began to stroke herself, the combination of her own touch and Henry's relentless pace brought her closer and closer to climax.

"Come for me, my dear," Henry growled, his eyes never leaving hers.

At his words, Mary exploded, waves of pleasure crashing through her body. Moments later, Henry followed suit, his own release filling her as he groaned her name.

As they clung to one another, their breathing ragged and their limbs entwined, Mary knew that she had entered an entirely new world of passion and pleasure – one she couldn't wait to explore further with the man who had opened her eyes to it all.

As the afterglow of their passionate encounter enveloped them, Mary and Henry lay tangled in the rumpled sheets, a sheen of sweat coating their bodies. The room was filled with the intoxicating scent of sex, a testament to the intensity of their union.

"Fuck, Mary," Henry panted, his chest heaving as he struggled to catch his breath. "You were incredible."

"Thank you, Sir," she replied softly, her voice laced with satisfaction. "I never knew I could feel this way."

"Neither did I," he admitted, brushing a damp strand of hair from her forehead. "Being with you has been...incomparable."

Mary traced her fingers over the patterns of perspiration on his chest, feeling the rapid beat of his heart beneath her touch. She marveled at how such a commanding man, who had just brought her to the brink of ecstasy through acts of dominance, could exhibit such tender vulnerability in these moments.

"Is it always like this?" she asked, her curiosity piqued.

"Between us? Yes," Henry said, his eyes locked onto hers. "But not everyone experiences the connection we have. It's unique, special."

"Like a hidden treasure," Mary whispered, her mind reeling with the possibilities that lay before them.

"Exactly," he agreed, pulling her closer to him. "And now that we've unlocked it, there's no going back."

"Promise me, Sir," she murmured, her fingertips tracing the contours of his face. "Promise me that this is only the beginning."

Henry caught her hand and pressed a lingering kiss to her palm. "I promise, Mary," he vowed, his voice resonating with sincerity. "This is only the first step in our journey together."

"Let's continue to explore our darkest fantasies together," Henry whispered into her ear, his breath hot against her skin. "From now on, we'll leave no stone unturned. We'll delve deeper into the realms of pleasure and pain, dominance and submission."

"Take me there, Sir," Mary murmured, her eyes shining with anticipation. "Show me everything."

"The next step is to show you a hidden world that you never knew existed. We will be attending a masquerade ball where everyone in attendance is as in tune with their sexual desires as we are. Are you ready for that?"

Mary hesitated.

"Yes, Henry. I am ready."

4

The opulent mansion loomed before Mary, a dazzling vision of grandeur and sensuality. Moonlight shimmered on the marble columns and arches, casting soft shadows on silk-draped walls adorned with artful frescoes of cherubs and nymphs. The chandeliers, dripping in crystal, cast a warm glow upon the decadent scene unfolding below.

Guests swirled around the ballroom floor, their extravagant costumes leaving little to the imagination. Men in tailored suits that hugged their powerful frames brushed up against women dressed in sheer gowns that clung to every curve, revealing the tantalizing secrets beneath.

Mary, clad in a sultry black corset and skirt, felt her heart race as she entered the fray. Henry's tall form was impeccably dressed in a dark suit that emphasized the strength of his broad shoulders.

"Mary," he murmured, his voice like liquid sin, "you look positively delicious." His eyes roved over her figure, lingering on the swell of her breasts above the corset's lace trim.

"Thank you, Henry," she replied breathlessly, feeling her

cheeks flush under the weight of his smoldering gaze. "You're quite dashing yourself."

"Shall we dance?" he asked, extending his hand, which she eagerly took, allowing him to lead her onto the dance floor. As they moved to the sultry rhythm of the waltz, his strong arm wrapped around her waist, pulling her close, so close she could feel the heat emanating from his body.

"Your scent is intoxicating," he whispered into her ear, sending shivers down her spine. "If I didn't know better, I'd think you were purposely trying to drive me mad with desire."

"Isn't that half the fun?" she teased, feeling a thrill of excitement as his grip on her waist tightened.

"Careful, my dear," he warned, his breath hot against her neck. "I'm not known for my restraint when it comes to beautiful women who toy with me."

"Is that a threat or a promise?" Mary challenged, looking up into his dark eyes, which seemed to burn with a fiery hunger.

"Perhaps both," he replied, his voice low and dangerous. His hand slid lower, resting on the curve of her ass, giving it a possessive squeeze that made her gasp.

"Please, Henry," she whispered, feeling her resolve crumble under the weight of his touch. "I need you."

"Patience," he murmured, pulling away just enough to look into her eyes, his expression filled with raw lust. "We have all night to explore each other's darkest desires. Let's make this a night we'll never forget."

Mary's heart pounded in her chest as she and Henry stepped away from the dance floor, their bodies still flushed from their passionate waltz. The opulent ballroom seemed to throb with the energy of its many guests, each one engaged in some form of hedonistic pleasure. Mary couldn't help but let her gaze wander, taking in the explicit sights that surrounded her.

To her left, a woman wearing little more than a sheer black

corset and thigh-high stockings was bent over a chaise lounge, her hands bound above her head. A man, his face concealed by a dark velvet mask, trailed a riding crop along the exposed curves of her body, eliciting gasps and moans of ecstasy. The rhythmic smacking sound each time the leather kissed her flesh sent shivers down Mary's spine.

"Oh," she whispered to herself, feeling a rush of heat between her thighs. "This is beyond anything I've ever imagined."

Across the room, a couple engaged in a passionate embrace, their mouths locked together as if they were trying to devour one another. Their hands explored every inch of each other's bodies, fingers slipping beneath silken garments in an unabashed display of lust. Mary felt a pang of jealousy – she yearned for Henry's touch, craved the intensity of their connection.

"God, what am I doing here?" Mary thought, clenching her hands into fists at her sides. "I shouldn't be enjoying this. I should be ashamed."

But as her eyes continued to roam, she spotted a group gathered around a young woman suspended from the ceiling by silk ropes. Her body was a canvas of intricate knots, each one strategically placed to both support and expose her. The woman's face was a portrait of pure bliss, her mouth open in a silent cry of pleasure as a man skillfully manipulated a flogger against her tender flesh.

"My God," Mary muttered under her breath, feeling her body tense with a mixture of arousal and trepidation. "What kind of place is this?"

"Are you alright, my dear?" Henry asked, noticing the conflict in her eyes.

"Y-yes," she stammered, trying to regain control over her racing thoughts. "It's just... all so overwhelming."

"Take a deep breath," he instructed, his voice calm and reassuring. "You don't have to participate in anything you're not comfortable with. Just allow yourself to experience it – to feel what it does to your body."

But as Mary tried to heed Henry's advice, she couldn't help but be drawn to the scene unfolding before her. A woman knelt before her masked lover, her lips wrapped around his thick cock, greedily swallowing him down as he gripped her hair tightly. The raw, primal nature of it struck something deep within her, threatening to consume her entirely.

"I want that," she thought, her chest tightening with shame and guilt. "I shouldn't want it, but I do."

"Remember, Mary," Henry murmured into her ear, as if reading her thoughts. "There's no judgment here. Only pleasure."

"Are you alright, Mary?" Henry's voice was gentle, his eyes filled with concern as he noticed her body trembling. The whirl-wind of carnal activities surrounding them was overwhelming her senses.

"Y-yes," she stammered, trying to focus on him and not the erotic scenes unfolding around them. "It's just so... intense."

"Would you like to step away for a moment? We can find a quieter corner to talk." His offer was comforting, and Mary nodded gratefully.

As they moved to a more secluded area, they could still hear the moans and gasps of pleasure echoing through the opulent mansion. They sat down on a plush velvet chaise, and Mary looked into Henry's eyes with vulnerability.

"Tell me what's on your mind," he urged gently, his fingers brushing against hers, sending shivers down her spine.

"I... I've never been exposed to anything like this before," she confessed, her cheeks flushing red in embarrassment. "I feel guilty for being aroused by it all."

"Mary, it's natural to be intrigued and aroused by new experiences," he reassured her, his voice soft and soothing. "You shouldn't feel guilty for your desires. This place is meant to explore our deepest fantasies without judgment."

"But what if I'm not... enough?" Her voice wavered as she voiced her insecurity. "What if my desires are too tame compared to everyone else's?"

Henry leaned toward her, their lips inches apart, his breath warm and intoxicating. "Your desires are uniquely yours, and that makes them beautiful," he whispered, his words igniting a fire within her. "No one here has the right to judge you or determine what is enough."

Their eyes met, and Mary saw the sincerity in his gaze. She felt her body responding to him, aching for his touch. With a newfound boldness, she asked, "Will you help me explore my desires, Henry?"

"Of course," he replied, his voice husky with anticipation. "What do you want to try first?"

"Kiss me." The words escaped her lips before she could second-guess herself.

He obliged, their mouths meeting in a passionate, hungry kiss. His tongue teased her own, and she felt a surge of arousal coursing through her veins. When they finally broke apart, breathless, Henry gazed into her eyes, the intensity of his desire evident.

"Let's find a room where we can be alone," he suggested, his hand sliding up her thigh, causing her heart to race with anticipation.

"Y-yes," she agreed, her body quivering with longing. "I want that."

As Mary and Henry made their way through the opulent halls of the mansion, they stumbled upon a dimly lit room where a group of guests gathered, engaged in various erotic activities. The scent of desire hung heavy in the air, mingling with the sweet aroma of expensive perfumes. The sight before her both intrigued and terrified Mary.

"Come," Henry whispered in her ear, his warm breath sending shivers down her spine. His hand gently guided her into the room, his touch comforting yet suggestive.

"Are you sure?" Mary hesitated, unable to tear her eyes away from the spectacle before her. Her heart raced as she watched a woman, clad in a leather corset and thigh-high boots, dominate a gentleman on his knees. She felt a pang of guilt for finding it so arousing.

"Trust me," Henry replied, his voice steady and reassuring. "We're just observers here."

As they stood there, taking in the sights and sounds of the hedonistic room, a tall, dark-haired man approached them. He wore a mask that obscured most of his face, but his eyes were piercing blue, and they seemed to undress Mary with a single glance. A sly grin played on his lips as he regarded the two of them.

"Good evening," he said, his voice deep and seductive. "I couldn't help but notice the beautiful lady standing here. Would you care for a dance?

Mary looked at Henry, seeking his approval. But as she glanced back at the mysterious man, she felt an undeniable attraction, a magnetic pull towards him. The temptation was strong, and she found herself conflicted.

"Go ahead," Henry whispered, his grip tightening around her waist. "I'll be right here, watching."

With a hesitant nod, Mary allowed the stranger to lead her to the center of the room. As they danced, the chemistry between them was palpable, their bodies moving in perfect synchrony. Mary's breath hitched as the man leaned in close, his lips brushing against her ear.

"Would you like to explore more...intimate pleasures with me?" he whispered, his voice dripping with seduction. "I can show you things you've never imagined."

Mary's heart pounded, torn between her newfound desire for Henry and the allure of this mysterious man. Just as she was about to give in to temptation, Henry stepped forward, pulling her away from the stranger's grasp. His eyes blazed with intensity, his hands possessive as they held her close.

"Mary," he said firmly, his voice laced with undisguised desire. "You don't need him to show you anything. I'm here for you, to explore and guide you through all your fantasies."

His words sent a wave of heat coursing through her body, reigniting her longing for him. She knew then that it was Henry she wanted, and only him. Together they left the room, their bond stronger than ever, ready to delve into the depths of their shared desires.

"Are you ready, Mary?" Henry asked, his voice deep and commanding. The intensity in his eyes was enough to make her knees weak.

"Y-yes," she stammered, her heart pounding with anticipation.

"Good," he purred, leading her into a hidden chamber adorned with lavish velvet drapes and plush cushions. A dim glow from flickering candles cast an intimate warmth over the room. "You're mine now, completely."

"Please, Henry," Mary whimpered, her desire for him consuming every fiber of her being. She wished nothing more than to submit to him.

"Undress," he ordered, watching as her trembling hands began to peel away the layers of her gown. As her body was slowly revealed, Henry's gaze consumed her, making her feel both vulnerable and desired.

"Come here," he beckoned, pulling her onto his lap. His fingers traced a trail of fire along her spine, igniting a passion that threatened to consume them both. "Do you trust me?"

"Completely," she breathed, her body aching for his touch.

"Then let's begin."

As Henry whispered filthily explicit instructions into Mary's ear, she found herself following his lead without question. He guided her through moments of pain and pleasure, binding her wrists with silk restraints and teasing her most sensitive areas with expert precision. The sharp crack of a riding crop against her flesh sent shivers of ecstasy down Mary's spine, her mind awash with sensations she never thought possible.

"Tell me what you want, Mary," Henry demanded, his breath hot against her ear as he continued to torment her body with his wickedly skilled hands.

"Fuck me, Henry," she gasped, desperate to be claimed by him. "Please... I need you inside me."

"Your wish is my command," he replied, a devilish smile playing on his lips as he positioned himself between her thighs. With a single, powerful thrust, he filled her completely, drawing forth an impassioned cry from Mary's lips.

"Y-yes, Henry!" she moaned, her body writhing beneath him as he set a punishing pace. Every stroke of his cock inside her sent waves of pleasure crashing through her, building to an intensity she'd never experienced before.

"Look at me," Henry commanded, his eyes locked onto hers as they moved together in a primal dance of passion. "Let me see you surrender."

In that moment, Mary felt herself truly let go, her body and mind wholly given over to the exquisite pleasure that Henry provided. Their cries of ecstasy rang out in unison as they reached their climax, their bodies trembling with the force of their release.

With that, they lay entwined in the flickering candlelight, their hearts beating in sync as they basked in the afterglow of their newfound connection.

5

Mary and Henry, hand in hand, exited the dimly lit mansion where the party had taken place. The night air was crisp and fragrant with the scent of roses from the nearby garden. Moonlight glinted off their sweat-slicked skin as they moved further away from the muffled sounds of pleasure and debauchery behind them. Their breaths came out in heavy pants, evidence of the wild romp they had just experienced within those walls.

"God, that was incredible," Mary exhaled, her voice still quivering from the intense release she had shared with Henry only moments before. Her body ached in all the right places, and she could feel the lingering tingle of her arousal between her thighs.

Henry's grip tightened around her hand and he pulled her close, pressing his lips hungrily against hers. Their tongues danced together in a passionate embrace, tasting the remnants of their earlier encounter. "I can't get enough of you, Mary," he murmured, his eyes dark with lust.

Mary leaned into him, feeling the heat of his body against hers and remembering how their bodies had become one. She recalled how he had expertly bound her wrists, teasing her with his skilled fingers and tongue, pushing her to the edge before finally plunging deep within her. She felt herself grow warm at the memory, a shiver racing down her spine.

"Tonight was amazing, Henry," she whispered, her eyes fixed on his, filled with desire and gratitude. "I'm so glad you came to my bookstore that day. I never thought our first encounter would lead us here, exploring our deepest fantasies together."

"Neither did I," he admitted, his voice thick with emotion. "But I wouldn't trade it for anything." He traced a finger along her jawline, admiring the way the moonlight played on her flushed cheeks. "You've opened up a whole new world for me, Mary."

They stood there for a moment, lost in each other's eyes, the memory of their wicked night replaying behind their eyelids. The intensity of their shared experiences had forged an intimate bond between them, one that went beyond just the physical pleasure they had found in each other's arms.

Hand in hand, they walked slowly toward their carriage, the night air cooling their heated skin, but unable to quench the burning desire that still smoldered between them. Their secret world of passion and exploration had only just begun, and they knew without a doubt that there were many more nights like this one to come.

"Mary," Henry began, his voice low and filled with a carnal hunger that sent shivers down her spine. "I can't get enough of you. I want us to continue our sexual journey... explore every dark, filthy corner of our desires." His hand tightened around hers, fingers interlacing as though they were about to embark on a thrilling adventure.

"Henry," she breathed, her pulse quickening at the thought of pushing their boundaries even further. "You're making my heart race just thinking about it."

He grinned wickedly, a devilish glint in his eyes. "Good.

Because I've got plans for you, darling. We'll start small – perhaps some voyeurism. We'll find an audience to appreciate our primal lusts."

"An audience?" Her breath hitched, her body buzzing with arousal at the mere thought of being watched, of becoming a living, breathing exhibition of pleasure.

"Absolutely. And from there, we'll dive deeper into the world of BDSM. Domination, submission, bondage... Every dirty little secret locked away in our minds will be set free, explored until we're both completely satisfied."

Her heart thudded wildly in her chest, her core throbbing with need as she listened to the sinful promises Henry spoke. It was as if he'd read her mind, tapped into the darkest depths, and brought forth all the fantasies she'd never dared to voice.

"Please, Henry... Let's do it. I want you to take control, tie me up, have your way with me," she whimpered, her voice breaking with the intensity of her longing.

"Patience, my dear," he murmured, his lips brushing against her ear as he whispered the words. "We have the rest of our lives to explore everything your body desires."

THE END

Printed in Great Britain
by Amazon

37278387R00020